To George, Digby and Harry

First published in 1989 in Great Britain by Aurum Books for Children
Published in this edition in 2001 by

CHILDREN'S BOOKS

Winchester House, 259-269 Old Marylebone Road,
London NW1 5XJ

1 3 5 7 9 10 8 6 4 2

Text and illustrations © Peter Utton 1989

The right of Peter Utton to be identified
as the author and illustrator of this work has been asserted by him
in accordance with the Copyright, Designs, and Patents Act, 1988.

A CIP record for this title is available from the British Library.

ISBN 1-86233-410-2

Printed and bound in China

The Witch's Hand

by
Peter Utton

GULLANE
CHILDREN'S BOOKS

"YIKES!" said George. "What's that?" and he
pointed to a horrible, brown, crinkly thing pinned to the wall.
    Dad looked up. "Oh, that, why that's a . . . " and he
paused and looked down at his son, "that's a . . . no,
I can't tell you – it's too scary."
    "Scary?" cried George. "Why is it scary? Tell me, tell me!"
    "Oh, all right then," said Dad, "but it is scary."
And he lifted George on to his lap.

"Well," said Dad, "last night when you and your brother and Mommy and I were all in bed, I woke up suddenly. I sat up and stared into the darkness. I heard a sort of

slither-slither

pat-pat

cackle-cackle.

Someone, or something, was moving down the hall.

I slipped out of bed and crept to the door.

Listening, I heard again the slithery-pattery-cackling sound coming closer.

I rushed on tiptoe to your bedroom. The door was slightly open. I peeped in. My hair stood on end and I gazed in horror as I saw a huge witch, dressed in a great black cloak and tall pointed hat, bending over your little beds.

By the dim glow of your nightlight I could see she was horribly ugly. She peered down at you with an awful grin, and from between her green, occasional teeth squeezed a grotesque cackle.

   She lifted up a dirty sack and, as her bony hand reached out towards you, I tried to shout, 'Stop! You horrible old hag!'

   But all I said was,

'STORRUGORRIGUGGUGAG . . .'

The witch stopped, slowly turned and fixed me with
a terrible bloodshot stare. Pointing a disgusting finger
at me she hissed a most evil hiss,

'Stand back – I must
have these boys!'

'Oh, no you won't!' I whispered and, staggering
over to her, I gripped her large warty wrists.
'Yuck!' I thought.
Just touching her made me shiver.

We struggled for many long minutes in a dreadful silence,
until I was able to grab her and give her a good shake.

'Uggle, oggle, aggle!'

she squawked and went limp and smelly.

'I've won!' I thought, but suddenly, with a blood-freezing cackle, the vile old woman began growing larger and stronger and more revolting by the second.

'Quiet!' called Mommy, poking her head round
the bedroom door. 'Don't wake the boys!'

'Quick!' I gasped. 'Get the sword!'

'Sword? Which sword?' asked Mommy.

'Yes, the witch sword. It's in the broom cupboard!' I said.

'Oh, that sword,' cried Mommy, and rushed from the room.

'You silly little man!' croaked the witch and, bending her
face down to mine, she blew a sickening cloud of stench
and cobwebs into my face, and grabbed me!

'This is the end!' I thought, but then Mommy
appeared in the doorway, wielding the great
sword from the broom cupboard.

'Too late!' hissed the witch and stabbed
at me with a dagger of vipers.

'Take that!' cried Mommy
and with one bound and a great swish of
the sword she cut off the horrible hand and
it fell to the ground with its fearful weapon.

'Not fair!' the witch screeched and, with
a squelchy-spluttery sound, she started to sink down and
down until, with a final, watery splop! she disappeared.

'Phew!' I said. 'That was close!' And Mommy
and I looked at you and your brother still
sleeping quietly in your beds.

'Look!' said Mommy, pointing at the floor.
There lay the horrible hag's hand, all brown
and withered and crinkly.

'I'll pin that on the wall,' I said, 'to remind me
to lock all the doors at night.'

'Good idea,' said Mommy. 'I'll make some tea.'

"And that's the story of the witch's hand," said Dad, and George gazed up at the horrible, brown, crinkly thing.

"Is that really the witch's hand?" he whispered.

"No," replied Dad, and he reached up and picked it off the wall. "It's a leaf I found in the park the other day. It was a beautiful, reddish-gold color but now it's gone all horrible and brown and crinkly," and he crushed it to dust in his hand and dropped it in the garbage can.

"It was just a story," he laughed.

George looked at the wall, and then he looked at the garbage can; then he looked at his Mommy and saw that she was smiling.

"What a scary story! Tell it again!" cried George, and then he laughed too.